W9-BBZ-285

Copyright © 2009 by NordSüd Verlag AG, Heinrichstrasse 249, CH-8005 Zürich, Switzerland.
First published in Switzerland under the title *Wenn du mal groß bist, Nils!*
English translation copyright © 2009 by North-South Books Inc., 350 Seventh Avenue, New York 10001.

Published in the United States, Great Britain, Canada, Australia, and New Zealand in 2009
by North-South Books Inc., an imprint of NordSüd Verlag AG, CH-8005 Zürich, Switzerland.
First paperback edition published in 2011 by North South Books Inc.
Distributed in the United States by North-South Books Inc., New York 10001.
Library of Congress Cataloging-in-Publication Data is available.
Printed in China by Leo Paper Products Ltd., Heshan, Guangdong, November 2010.
ISBN: 978-0-7358-2224-5 (hardcover edition)
1 3 5 7 9 HC 10 8 6 4 2
ISBN 978-0-7358-4005-8 (paperback)
1 3 5 7 9 PB 10 8 6 4 2

www.northsouth.com

Bertie:
Just Like Daddy

Marcus Pfister

NorthSouth
New York / London

Bertie and Daddy are having breakfast.

"Drink your milk, Bertie," says Daddy.

"I want coffee," says Bertie. "Just like you."

"Coffee is for grown-ups," says Daddy.

"You'll have to wait until you're bigger."

"I'm bigger already," says Bertie.

"Indeed you are!" Daddy laughs.

"I think you're big enough for some of the foam."

"I want to read the newspaper," says Bertie.

"Just like you."

"You'll learn to read when you're bigger," says Daddy.

"Right now, you're just the right size

for a paper hat."

"I want to shave," says Bertie.

"Just like you."

"Will you settle for some shaving cream?"

Daddy asks.

"Give me a white beard," says Bertie.

"Let's ride our bike to the store," says Daddy.

"I want to steer," says Bertie. "Just like you."

"When you're bigger, you'll have your own bike,"
says Daddy. "With room for me on the back."

Bertie gets to push the shopping cart.

He helps Daddy fill it with oranges

and cornflakes and vegetables and something sweet.

At the checkout, Daddy pays with his card.

"I want a card too!" shouts Bertie.

"Just like you!"

"When you grow up,

you can have a credit card," says Daddy.

"Right now, you can carry the receipt."

Bertie helps unpack the bags.

Then Daddy starts to cook.

"I want to cook too," says Bertie.

"Just like you."

"When you're older,

you'll be a great cook," says Daddy.

"Right now, you're a great taster."

Bertie gets the knives and forks.

He sets the table.

Then he gets the salad bowl.

"That's a big bowl for a little boy," says Daddy.

"I can do it!" says Bertie.

"So you can!" says Daddy.

"I want to play before lunch," says Bertie.

"Nope," says Daddy. "It's time to eat now."

"I always have to do what *you* say," says Bertie.

"When I'm bigger, we have to do what *I* say."

"Right," says Daddy.

After lunch, it's time for a nap.

"*You* don't have to nap," says Bertie.

"I want to stay up—just like you."

"When you're older,

you won't have to nap anymore," says Daddy.

He carries Bertie piggyback to bed.

"Sleep tight," says Daddy.

"I'm not sleeping," says Bertie.

When Bertie wakes up, he plays with his train.

"Can I play too?" Daddy asks.

"I'm sorry," says Bertie. "You're too grown up."

"I want to be a kid," says Daddy. "Just like you."

"Well, all right," says Bertie.

"But I'm the engineer."